123

Library of Congress Cataloging-in-Publication Data:
Cross, Molly. Wait for me! (A Sesame Street start-to-read book) SUMMARY: Elmo is just too small and too slow to keep up with his bigger friends on Sesame Street, but a treat from Grover's grandpa demonstrates that sometimes it can be good not to rush off. [1. Size—Fiction. 2. Speed—Fiction. 3. Grandfathers—Fiction. 4. Puppets—Fiction]
I. Mathieu, Joseph, ill. II. Title. III. Series: Sesame Street start-to-read books. PZ7.C88273Wai 1987 [E]
87-12926 ISBN: 0-394-89135-X (trade); 0-394-99135-4 (lib. bdg.)

Manufactured in the United States of America   2 3 4 5 6 7 8 9 0

WAIT FOR ME!

by Molly Cross • illustrated by Joe Mathieu

Featuring Jim Henson's Sesame Street Muppets

Random House/Children's Television Workshop

Elmo was younger and smaller
than all of his friends
on Sesame Street.
It was hard for him
to keep up with them.

Elmo could not run
as fast as the others.

He could not jump
as far as the others.

He could not play baseball at all.
The bat was bigger than Elmo!

One sunny day Ernie and Bert
and Big Bird and Grover
went roller skating in the park.
Elmo went too.

Suddenly a bell rang.

It was the ice cream truck.

Everyone skated off

to get some ice cream.

"Hey!" Elmo cried. "Wait for me!"

Grover skated back to Elmo.

"I, Grover, will help you.

Hold on to my hand," he said.

And off they went.

Clickety-clack, lickety-split,
faster and faster they went…

until they hit a bump.
CRASH! They both fell down.

"WAH! WAH!" went Elmo.

"Oh, my goodness! Are you hurt?"
asked Grover.

"I have a boo-boo on my leg,"
cried Elmo.

Grover looked and looked.

At last he found a tiny scratch.

"Do not cry," said Grover.

"We are near my house.

We can go there

and wash your scratch."

On the way they saw

Ernie and Bert and Big Bird.

They were eating ice cream.

But the ice cream truck was gone.

"Where were you?" asked Big Bird.

"Helping Elmo," Grover said sadly.

"We're going to get our bikes now,"
said Ernie.

"Do you want to go biking with us?"
Bert asked Grover.

"Oh, yes," said Grover.

"After I take care of Elmo."

Grover took Elmo to his bathroom.

He washed Elmo's tiny scratch.

He put a tiny bandage on it.

Then he said to Elmo,

"I am going biking now."

Elmo said, "Me too!"

"No, Elmo. You are too little,"
said Grover.

Elmo looked sad.

"Will I be big enough tomorrow?"
he asked Grover.

"I do not think so," said Grover.

Grover took his bike outside.
Elmo sadly watched
Grover ride off.

"Everybody is bigger and faster
and better at everything,"
said Elmo to himself.
"Not me!" said a kind voice.

It was Grover's grandpa.
"I know how you feel, Elmo,"
he said. "But sometimes fun things
happen when you are left behind.
How would you like to go to the zoo
with me this afternoon?
I was going to ask Grover,
but he was in such a rush
to go biking.
How about it, Elmo?"
Elmo began to smile.
"Yes!" he said happily.

At the zoo they watched
the zoo keeper feed the seals.

Then Grandpa bought some peanuts.
"Now let's feed the elephants,"
he said.
And they did.

After they saw all the animals,
Grandpa said, "Time to go home."
Elmo said, "Take me home piggyback?"
Grandpa shook his head.
"No, Elmo," he said.
"I am just as tired as you are."

As soon as they got back
to Grover's house,
Grandpa sat down.
He took off his shoes.
"Oh, that feels good," he said.

"Elmo, you're just the right size
to sit on my lap
and listen to a story.
So come on up here," said Grandpa.
Elmo climbed up on Grandpa's lap
and listened to Grandpa read
the story of "The Three Bears."

"And they lived happily ever after,"
said Grandpa.
Just then Grover came in.
"Who lived happily ever after?"
asked Grover, who was surprised
to see Elmo in his grandpa's lap.

"The Three Bears, the Three Bears!"
shouted Elmo. "And guess what?
We saw REAL bears!"
Now Grover was really surprised.
"What? Where did you see real bears?"
cried Grover.
"At the zoo," said Elmo.

"You went to the zoo without me?"
wailed Grover.
"We saw the zoo keeper
feed the seals," said Elmo.
"And we fed the elephants.
Oh, we had so much fun!

"And we had an ice cream cone!"
"What kind?" Grover asked.
"Chocolate chip with sprinkles!"
said Elmo.

"Grover dear,
   did you have fun
   riding your bike?"
   asked his grandpa.
"Oh, yes," said Grover.

"But Grandpa, next time
you go to the zoo,
will you please wait for me?"